PONY DAYS

SHELTIE in Double Trouble

PONY DAYS

SHELTIE in Double Trouble

by Peter Clover

Cover illustration by
Tristan Elwell

AN
APPLE
PAPERBACK

SCHOLASTIC INC.
New York Toronto London Auckland Sydney
Mexico City New Delhi Hong Kong Buenos Aires

ISBN 0-439-68490-0

12 11 10 9 8/0

Printed in the U.S.A. 40

First Scholastic printing, September 2004

To Marilyn and Howard

PONY DAYS

SHELTIE in Double Trouble

Chapter One

Sheltie the Shetland pony was waiting patiently in his paddock for Emma to give him his breakfast. He blew noisily through his nostrils and rippled his lips in an almost silent raspberry.

"Come on, boy. Here it is."

Emma arrived and scooped his pony mix into the feed manger. Sheltie immediately gobbled it all up.

"Anyone would think I haven't fed you for days," said Emma.

Within seconds, he had eaten all the pony nuts and was looking for more.

Sheltie sniffed the empty manger, then watched Emma put some fresh hay in the rack on the back wall of his field shelter. The little pony pulled a huge clump free and stood with it hanging from his mouth like a long, golden beard. He *did* look funny.

Emma giggled as she kissed his soft velvet nose.

"Oh, Sheltie." She laughed. "You're such a clown! You ought to be in a circus!"

Sheltie answered by shaking his

head quickly and showered Emma with hay.

"That's for eating. Not for throwing at me!" scolded Emma with a smile.

The little Shetland pony peered at Emma through his shaggy forelock, then nibbled at the spilled hay as Emma went inside for her own breakfast.

As she ran up the path toward the house, Mr. Crock came ambling along the lane with his wheelbarrow.

"Good morning, Emma," called the elderly man as he waved across the top of the garden wall. "I see you've got Sheltie back safe and sound!"

Then he hurried off on his way without another word.

Emma was puzzled. What did Mr. Crock

mean? Of course Sheltie was safe and sound. He hadn't been anywhere!

Emma finished her cereal and sat at the kitchen table thinking about what Mr.

Crock had said. But she soon forgot all about it when Mom asked her if she would run a few errands.

Emma liked errands. Especially when she could take Sheltie along with her. Sheltie loved poking his head into all the shops along the way.

"I've made a list of things I need from town," said Mom. "You could tie my wicker basket to Sheltie's saddle if you like. You can be a Shetland shopper!"

Emma liked that idea. She took Mom's list and stuffed the errand money into the pocket of her jeans.

"We'll be the best-looking shoppers in Little Applewood," said Emma.

Mom laughed. "There's no need to rush, though," she said. "It's Saturday and you've got all morning. Just cross everything off the list as you buy it and come home when you've finished."

"I will," said Emma. "And I promise I won't forget anything!"

Outside in the paddock, Emma tacked up Sheltie in record time. Mom came out with the wicker basket and tied it to the little pony's saddle.

Joshua, Emma's little brother, wanted to know what was going on. "Where's Sheltie going?" he asked.

"Sheltie and I are off to run some errands," said Emma. "See you later," she called as she swung her leg up and over the saddle. Then she turned Sheltie into the road, flicked his reins, and headed off toward the town.

As Emma trotted Sheltie over the little stone bridge at the end of the road, she passed Marjorie Wallace coming back from the stores.

"I see you've got Sheltie back," said Marjorie, giving a little wave as she hurried along with her shopping bags.

Emma wondered what she meant. But the elderly woman was in such a rush, she had disappeared down the path before Emma could ask.

"That's what Mr. Crock said, Sheltie! What do they mean about getting you back? You haven't been anywhere, have you?"

Sheltie jangled his bit and shook his reins. He didn't seem to know what was going on, either.

Emma tethered Sheltie before going into all the stores, one by one, and buying everything on Mom's list. Sheltie poked his head into each store's doorway as Emma went in, and then stood patiently outside on High Street.

At last, Emma finished her errands.

The little pony snorted happily as she packed the last bag into her wicker basket.

"All the errands are done, Sheltie," said Emma. "Now we can go home."

But Sheltie didn't seem to want to go home. He enjoyed waiting outside the stores while Emma was inside. Lots of people had come up to fuss over him. And outside Mr. Samson's candy shop, Emma had overheard them saying things like, "So you're safely back with Emma, Sheltie!" and "You little rascal! Eating all of Mrs. Marsh's marigolds!"

Sheltie didn't understand what they were saying, but he obviously liked all the attention.

Emma, on the other hand, didn't have a clue what was going on. What was everyone talking about? But it was only when she was riding Sheltie home that Emma started to think that something really funny was happening.

They had just left town and were clip-clopping toward the bridge when they were stopped by Mrs. Price, the principal's wife.

"Hello, Emma!" she said brightly, suddenly popping out of her house and shutting the door. "I hope Sheltie's feeling all right after all those plums he gobbled up earlier!"

"Plums!" exclaimed Emma. "Sheltie hasn't eaten any plums. He's been with me all morning and hasn't been near a plum!"

Mrs. Price laughed. "Well, ponies will be ponies," she said. "I saw him with my own eyes. And I know what I saw." Then she set off toward town.

"What's going on, Sheltie? What have you been up to?" asked Emma. Sheltie blew a long raspberry and swished his tail. Just like Emma, he didn't seem to have a clue.

Chapter Two

As they rode home down the road, Emma thought about what Mrs. Price had said.

"Plums! *Have* you had any plums today, Sheltie? You haven't sneaked out and been walking around — or eating around, have you?"

Sheltie shook his mane as if to say, "No."

"Then I don't know what's going on," said Emma, feeling very confused.

Minutes later, as she rode up to the house with the groceries, Emma found Mom waiting for her. She was standing on

the back step looking puzzled. Joshua was with her, pulling at her sleeve.

"Sheltie, bad!" he said. "Bad, bad." Then he giggled and jumped up and down as Emma unpacked the basket.

"I just had a very strange phone call," Mom told Emma. "Do you remember Mrs. Warner, the elderly lady who lives out on the hill? Well, she called to say that she saw Sheltie running across the fields, all on his own. She thought maybe he had escaped and that we would be worried! She also said that Mrs. Marsh had seen him eating flowers from her window box."

"Flowers!" exclaimed Emma. "But Sheltie doesn't eat flowers. Something really funny is going on!" Then she told

Mom what Mr. Crock, Marjorie Wallace, and Mrs. Price had said about Sheltie.

"I don't understand it, but I don't like these mysteries," said Mom. "Mysteries like this usually mean that you and Sheltie end up having an adventure!"

"We haven't had an adventure for ages," said Emma, grinning. Sheltie scuffed his hoof in the dusty earth and disturbed a beetle. The little pony sniffed at the insect as it tried to scurry away.

"No, Sheltie," warned Emma, "leave the beetle alone."

"Perhaps you'd better stick to plums and flowers, Sheltie," said Mom with a grin.

"But Sheltie's innocent," cried Emma. "He hasn't eaten any plums or flowers. How could he have? He's been safely locked in his paddock since we came home yesterday afternoon. And the paddock's escape-proof. Dad said so!"

"I wouldn't be so sure about that." Mom laughed. "When Sheltie is determined to do something, anything can happen. We'll just have to keep a careful eye on him!"

In the kitchen, at lunchtime, Emma described the mystery to Dad.

"Maybe there's another pony out there that looks just like Sheltie," Dad suggested. "A mystery pony, running wild around Little Applewood."

Emma laughed. "There isn't another pony in the whole world that looks like Sheltie," she said. She sneaked a piece of apple into her pocket to give Sheltie as a treat later on.

"I don't know about that," teased Dad. "Lots of ponies look alike. And I'm sure there probably *is* another Shetland pony somewhere in the world that looks like Sheltie."

"There might be another Shetland somewhere that looks a little like Sheltie," said Emma confidently, "but not one that looks exactly the same. And if there was, I would still be able to tell them apart. I'd know Sheltie anywhere!"

But the next day, when Emma was out riding, she got a big surprise.

It was Sunday afternoon and the Matthews family had just finished a delicious lunch. Dad was busy washing up and Mom was snoozing on the sofa, with little Joshua sprawled among the cushions.

"I think I'll take Sheltie out for a gallop," announced Emma. "It's such a nice afternoon and it would be a shame to waste all that sunshine."

Within minutes, she had tacked up Sheltie and they were heading out toward the fields.

Golden sunlight bounced off Sheltie's mane as he danced along, squashing the soft, spongy grass beneath his hoofs. Emma let Sheltie canter freely wherever he wanted to go.

Sheltie flicked his tail and drew a deep breath of fresh air through his nostrils. He turned sideways, but stopped suddenly — the little pony was staring hard across the fields at an animal coming toward them.

Emma glanced across to where Sheltie was looking. As the animal drew nearer, she could see it was another Shetland pony. And Emma could hardly believe her eyes. If she didn't know better, she would have sworn that it was Sheltie galloping toward them!

The pony was the same size and the same color as Sheltie. His mane and tail were the same length. And as he trotted nearer, Emma saw that he even had the same shaggy forelock. This Shetland pony, wherever he came from, was Sheltie's exact double!

As the pony approached, Sheltie blew a

loud greeting and rumbled a gentle whicker through his lips.

The stranger answered by snorting softly and rubbed noses with Sheltie. Then the two ponies made soft, snuffling noises to each other and Emma was certain that they were talking.

She sat in the saddle, watching in

amazement. There *was* another pony just like Sheltie, and he was standing right in front of them!

Emma slipped out of the saddle for a closer look. The mystery pony seemed happy to let her check him over. Her touch was friendly and confident. Emma had a good look at the pony's teeth, ears, legs, and hooves.

"I can't believe it," said Emma finally. "Whoever you are, you're exactly like Sheltie. Even *I* would have trouble telling you apart! Double trouble!" she said with a laugh.

Suddenly, without warning, the mystery pony kicked up his heels and took off at a frisky pace. He had been standing still long enough. Now he wanted to gallop across the fields.

Sheltie followed, eager to join in.

"Oh, no," groaned Emma. She certainly didn't want Sheltie running off with a strange pony.

But he did!

Chapter Three

Emma watched Sheltie disappear in a cloud of rising dust. His horseshoes glistened silver in the late afternoon sunlight as he kicked up his heels and galloped away.

"Sheltie!" yelled Emma. But her little pony didn't seem to hear. He just kept running.

Then something funny happened. Sheltie's double turned a neat circle and came running back toward Emma. Emma kept calling, "Sheltie, Sheltie!" and the mystery pony ran right up to her.

The real Sheltie followed, then nudged the look-alike out of the way as Emma reached out to ruffle his forelock.

Sheltie closed his eyes and whickered softly as Emma scratched his ears. The other pony cocked his head to one side and watched.

Emma smiled. "The mystery pony might *look* exactly like you, Sheltie," she told him, "but there's something very special about *my* Sheltie."

There was only *one* Sheltie, and Emma would always be able to pick him out.

Suddenly, the other pony ran off across the fields. This time Sheltie didn't follow. He turned his head and watched his new friend disappear. But he didn't run off. He stayed with Emma.

"Good boy," cooed Emma. She rubbed Sheltie's neck hard, then gathered the reins and swung up into the saddle. "Come on," she whispered in his ear. "Let's go home."

But when they reached home, they got another big surprise.

Waiting in Sheltie's paddock, with his fuzzy chin resting on the top rail of the wooden fence, was the strange pony.

Sheltie tossed his mane excitedly and blew a deafening snort. Then he pawed at the ground and stamped his feet, eager to greet his new friend.

"How did *you* get here?" exclaimed Emma. The mystery pony from the fields looked at Emma from beneath his shaggy fringe and blew a soft whicker.

Emma quickly glanced around the edge of the paddock fence. As far as she could see, nothing was broken. The fence was secure and the gate was closed. Emma looked again. "Maybe there is a loose post or something," she said. But nothing was loose. Emma couldn't understand how the Sheltie look-alike could have turned up in the paddock. It was another mystery.

Emma unlocked the pasture gate, took off Sheltie's tack, and turned him out into the paddock to play with his new friend. As soon as Emma pulled off his saddle, Sheltie was off! The little pony seemed delighted to have a playmate to run and gallop with. He kicked up his heels and ran to join his new friend in a mad gallop around the pasture.

Mom came down from the house and gasped when she saw the two ponies in Sheltie's paddock.

"What's going on? Where did the other pony come from?" she said as she watched the two ponies gallop around the little field. "Which one is Sheltie?"

Emma explained what had happened. She told Mom how they had found the look-alike pony out in the fields.

"I've never seen anything quite like it!" exclaimed Mom. "They're exactly alike!"

"He just appeared out of nowhere!" said Emma. "Sheltie made friends right away. And now it looks as though his new pony friend has come for a visit!"

"But how did he get into Sheltie's paddock?" wondered Mom. "The fence isn't damaged. And unless that pony is a champion show jumper, he couldn't have jumped the rails!"

It was true. The fence was far too high for a little Shetland pony to jump. Emma was puzzled.

After Mom went back inside, she decided to check the fencing up close.

Emma looked at it carefully. Sheltie studied it, too, and stared at the wooden rails.

There was a section of Sheltie's paddock that ran close to a raised bank. The earth here was built up into a ridge where the ground level was raised by at least a foot and a half. It was only a small mound of grass, but enough to provide a way into the paddock.

Emma decided that the pony could have jumped over the fence into the paddock if he had jumped from the bank. *He's a smart pony,* thought Emma. *Just like Sheltie!*

Chapter Four

Emma was feeling really pleased that she had figured out how the new pony had gotten into Sheltie's paddock. She smiled across at the two ponies as they chased each other in circles. From that distance, Emma couldn't tell the two Shetlands apart.

Suddenly, both ponies turned and looked at Emma. Then they thundered toward her at a fast gallop, with their shaggy manes flying.

Emma had just decided which one was *her* Sheltie when she realized that the frisky look-alike was not slowing down at all. He just kept galloping, straight at the fence.

"He's not going to stop," Emma said breathlessly. "He's going to try to jump!" She was afraid he might hurt himself, so she waved and flapped her arms across the top of the fence. Emma had learned from Farmer Brown that this worked with charging sheep. She only hoped that it would have the same effect on a galloping pony.

For one brief moment, Emma thought that she had succeeded. The pony suddenly moved to the left. But then it immediately turned in a full circle and came galloping back again.

"You silly thing!" yelled Emma. "The fence is far too high." But the pony obviously didn't think so.

At the last minute, Emma ducked out of the way. But the pony didn't jump after all. He turned again, only this time much closer to the fence. And as he turned, he kicked out with all the strength in his hind legs.

Emma gasped as the top rail of the fence flew clean off and went sailing through the air.

Then the pony came back again, only this time he *did* jump. He flew over the broken fence like a bird and galloped away.

Sheltie watched as the pony jumped the fence and came cantering over to investigate. Emma thought he was going to jump, too, and follow the mischievous pony up the road. But he didn't.

Sheltie stopped short and studied the broken rail. Then he shook his mane and blew a disgruntled snort.

"I know!" said Emma. "Just look what he's done to your fence."

She stroked Sheltie's face as she looked around for the broken rail. Sheltie looked, too, and gave a funny snort that sounded like a hiccup.

"Looks like Dad's got an emergency repair job now." Emma sighed. "I can't have *you* running away, Sheltie."

Sheltie blew a raspberry and his eyes twinkled with mischief.

"Please be good while I go get Dad. And don't move!" she warned. "I hope I can trust you, Sheltie!"

The little pony harrumphed gruffly, as if to say, "Of course you can trust me."

But when Emma came back out of the house a few minutes later, she couldn't find Sheltie anywhere.

At first, Emma thought he was just messing around and hiding in his field shelter. She called and called for the little pony, but he didn't show himself.

Emma had only been gone for a few moments. She couldn't believe that Sheltie would run as soon as her back was turned. But he obviously had, because the little pony was nowhere to be seen.

Emma rushed out into the road. She quickly looked both ways, down toward Mr. Brown's farm and Horseshoe Pond, then up the road toward town. She looked again, not knowing which way to go. Then she heard a distant neighing. It was Sheltie. Emma was sure of it. And it was coming from the town end of the road. Sheltie was calling to her. Something must be wrong.

Without wasting a second, Emma started running. Her feet barely touched the ground as she flew up the road, past Mr. Crock's house, toward town.

As she ran around the corner, Emma saw Sheltie up ahead. But he wasn't alone. Sheltie was being led away in a halter by a teenage girl.

"Stop!" yelled Emma. "Leave Sheltie alone." She covered the last few feet like a rocket.

When Sheltie heard Emma's voice, he dug in his hoofs and stopped in his tracks. Then he stamped his feet and grunted. The girl stopped, too, and turned her head. She looked really surprised when she saw Emma racing toward her.

"What do you think you're doing?" yelled Emma. "You can't just walk off with other people's ponies."

The girl looked puzzled. "I'm sorry," she said. "I don't know what you mean."

"Sheltie," said Emma. "You're stealing my Sheltie!"

"Sheltie!" exclaimed the girl. "This isn't Sheltie. This is Topper. He's been missing for two days and now I've finally found him."

Emma's mouth dropped open in disbelief.

"No!" she said. "This is Sheltie and he's *my* pony."

"But this *has* to be Topper," argued the girl. "I'd know him anywhere."

"Well, it's *not* Topper," insisted Emma. She suddenly realized that this girl must be the owner of the mystery pony. "This is Sheltie," she said. "Your pony, Topper, or whatever you call him, looks exactly like Sheltie. I've seen him in the fields and he's almost identical. But this is Sheltie."

Sheltie looked up at the girl and blew a loud raspberry.

"Does Topper do that?" said Emma, grinning.

The girl laughed. "No, he doesn't," she admitted. "So I guess you're right. This isn't Topper after all."

Emma smiled.

The girl was very apologetic. "I'm really sorry," she said. "I saw Topper, I mean

Sheltie, in the paddock, and I thought I'd found our missing runaway. We're campers, just passing through Little Applewood. Our Shetland pony escaped two days ago and ran off. I really thought this pony was our Topper."

Sheltie shook his head from side to side, whipping his cheeks with his long mane.

"You must think I'm terrible," said the girl, "just walking off with your pony like that. When I saw him in the paddock, I thought someone had put him in there for safekeeping."

Emma wasn't angry anymore. She now realized that the girl had made a big mistake. In fact, Emma felt sorry for her. She knew how awful *she* would feel if Sheltie got lost.

Chapter Five

"It's very easy to get Sheltie and Topper mixed up," said Emma. "They *do* look alike. I couldn't believe it when I first saw them together. They're like twins!" she added.

"They must be identical!" exclaimed the girl. She told Emma her name was Toyah and that she liked ponies.

Sheltie blew a loud snort and nuzzled her arm.

"And he didn't complain or resist when I slipped on the halter," Toyah continued, "so I thought he *must* be Topper."

"Sheltie's very friendly," said Emma, "and he likes you. That's why he let you take him for a walk."

"But where did you see Topper?" asked Toyah.

"We first met him up in the fields," Emma told her. "Then he turned up again in Sheltie's paddock. He was there just ten minutes ago, playing with Sheltie. But then he jumped clean over the fence. After knocking the top rail off," she added.

"That's one of his favorite tricks," said the girl. "They taught him how to do that when he was in the circus. He knows lots of other tricks, too. We rescued Topper when the circus broke up and all the animals were sold off."

"A circus," murmured Emma. Sheltie pricked up his ears, too. "Did Topper really come from a circus?"

The girl smiled. It was a warm, friendly smile. "Yes!" she beamed. "That's why he's so mischievous. He knows too many tricks."

"And I thought Sheltie was a handful," said Emma.

"Believe me," said the girl, smiling, "compared with Topper, your Sheltie is *very* well behaved."

Toyah slipped off the halter and Emma began leading Sheltie back down the road by holding on to his mane.

"If you do see Topper again," the

girl called after them, "will you please let me know so I can try to catch him? We're staying up on the North Field for at least another day before we have to move on."

"I'll try," Emma called back. She felt worried. What would happen to Topper if Toyah had to leave without him?

Back in the paddock, Dad was already busy nailing the wooden rail back in place.

"Where have you two been?" he said, looking up from the fence.

Emma unlocked the gate and led Sheltie into his pasture. Then she told Dad all about Sheltie's lucky escape.

"Five more minutes," said Emma, "and Sheltie would have been gone!"

At that moment, the little pony crept up and nudged Emma in the back as if to say, "But I'm still here, aren't I!" Emma threw her arms around his neck and gave him a big hug.

"It sounds like Toyah made an honest mistake," said Dad. "But it was lucky for Sheltie that you found him when you did. Who knows where he could have ended up!"

Sheltie harrumphed and blew a gentle snort. He seemed to know they were talking about him.

"Yes!" said Emma. "You could have been lost forever, couldn't you, boy?"

The little pony closed his eyes and

nuzzled Emma's arm. "I couldn't bear it if anything happened to you, Sheltie," she whispered.

"Well, I've fixed his fence now," said Dad. "So there's no way *our* pony is going to escape. And if this Topper shows up again, then we'll just catch him and return him to the campers."

But Emma thought that catching Topper could be a very tricky job.

Chapter Six

The next day, Emma didn't want to go to school. She was too worried about Sheltie.

Emma knew that her little pony couldn't escape from his paddock. She had already checked Sheltie's fence three times and found everything secure.

But she also knew that Topper was still out there somewhere. Emma didn't know whether he had found his own way home, been caught and led back to the campers' site, or was running free. But either way, Emma had a funny feeling about leaving Sheltie alone.

After scooping his pony mix into the feed manger, she watched Sheltie munch his breakfast and lick the sides clean, looking for more. Emma was very tempted to give him a small, extra handful. But she felt like that every day and she didn't want a pony as fat as a barrel, no matter how much she loved him.

Instead, she tore him off a handful of feed from the hay net and gave him the sweet, fresh food.

All day long at school, Emma couldn't think about anything else but Sheltie. At lunchtime, she rushed home to check that everything was all right. And in the afternoon, when school had finished, she flew down the road to the house, half expecting something to be wrong. But everything was OK. Sheltie was fine.

She took the little pony for a late ride and settled Sheltie down for the night in his paddock, feeling much better.

But later that evening, in her bedroom, Emma started worrying again. It took her ages to fall asleep. And when she did finally sink into sleep, she dreamed of mysterious dark strangers trying to lead Sheltie away.

When morning came, Emma woke to the sound of her alarm clock ringing.

Brrrrrinnnnggg!!! Emma sat bolt upright in bed.

"Sheltie!" she cried. She flew out of bed and raced to the window.

With a big sigh of relief, Emma saw Sheltie out in the paddock, waiting where he always did, with his fuzzy chin resting on the top bar of the paddock fence.

She hurried downstairs to give Sheltie

his breakfast. And *this* morning, she *did* give him an extra little handful of pony nuts.

Sheltie looked up from the empty feed manger and gave a loud belch.

"Manners, please!" said Emma, grinning. She threw her arms around his head and squeezed the little pony's neck.

"Now you be good, Sheltie," she said. "And make sure you're still here when I get home from school."

Then Emma felt a little silly. Of course Sheltie would be there. There was nowhere he could go. Nowhere he could escape from. But just to be on the safe side, Emma checked the paddock fencing twice.

Sheltie watched Emma go off to school. As she turned and waved to him one last time, Sheltie tossed back his head and whinnied. Then he sniffed and snuffled around the fence posts, hunting out dandelions.

But after a few mouthfuls, Sheltie got bored. The little pony scraped at the grass with his hoof, then nudged at the newly repaired top rail with his muzzle.

Sheltie cocked his head to one side. It was almost as if he was planning something.

Then the little pony twitched and flicked his tail and trotted in a circle around the paddock. As he passed the section of fence that Topper had kicked down to escape, Sheltie circled again. Only this time he broke into a fast canter. And when he passed the fence for the third and final time, he was racing at a full gallop.

Sheltie rushed at the fence, just as Topper had done, turning at the last moment, then kicking out with his hind legs. The little pony whinnied triumphantly as his hooves sent the top rail flying off through the air with the sound of splintering wood.

Sheltie stood for a moment with his neck hooked over the lower rail.

Sheltie could easily jump this lower rail. He backed up a few paces to take a run at it.

The next moment, Sheltie was trotting happily along the road. And nobody had seen him go.

Chapter Seven

Normally, the very first thing that Emma did when she got home from school was to rush over to Sheltie and feed him a carrot treat. Every day, she took a carrot to school in her backpack, and had it ready for her little Shetland pony the moment she reached the paddock. But today Emma was carrying a huge cage with a gerbil inside.

"I'll be with you in a minute, Sheltie," called Emma from across the yard. "I've just got to take Herbert inside. I'm looking after him for half the school year."

Emma went into the kitchen.

"Oh, hello, Emma," said Mom. "Would you just help me put these flyers into envelopes, please? They're to tell people about the craft fair this weekend. I've spent all afternoon printing them on my computer for Mrs. Hamilton at the shop, and now I'm all behind."

Emma put down the gerbil cage and sat at the kitchen table, opposite Mom.

"I can fold them, too," Emma said with a smile.

"I was going to ask you if you would deliver them for me as well, while I go to

Rilchester with Joshua to pick Dad up from the station," said Mom. "You could take Sheltie for a nice ride. He's been sad all day, so he's sulking in his field shelter."

"He's sad!" exclaimed Emma as she stuffed another flyer into an envelope. "And sulking! What's he been up to?"

Mom raised an eyebrow and told Emma how Sheltie had escaped.

"He picked up the trick from that circus pony, Topper," she began. "He kicked the same top rail off his paddock fence. I don't know how long he'd been out, but Mr. Crock brought him back after Sheltie showed up in his vegetable garden.

"Mr. Crock kindly nailed the rail back for me," Mom continued. "I've been in and out all afternoon checking on him," she groaned. "That's the other reason why I'm behind. In the end, I decided to tether him inside his shelter."

"Sheltie knows he's been bad," said Emma. "That's why he's sulking. Don't worry, Mom," she said, smiling. "I'll take Sheltie and deliver all your flyers."

But when Emma finished stuffing the

envelopes and went outside, there was a nasty surprise waiting for her.

She'd emptied her backpack and put all the flyers inside, ready for delivery. Then she went to the tack room for Sheltie's saddle and bridle.

"Sheltie!" called Emma as she bounced her way through the grass, toward the field shelter.

"Sheltie, you bad boy!" Emma scolded. She wasn't nearly as angry as she was pretending to be. Emma could never stay mad at Sheltie for long. It wasn't his fault that he was mischievous — that was what made him Sheltie. And Emma loved him.

The moment he heard Emma's voice, the little pony poked his head out of the shelter and answered with a welcoming whinny.

And *that* was when Emma realized that something wasn't quite right. She called again, "Sheltie, Sheltie, Sheltie," in her singsong way, as she hurried along. The little pony tossed his mane and blew a deep snort.

"Sheltie?" said Emma. "You sound funny!"

Emma stroked his furry face and ran her fingers over the velvet muzzle. She ruffled his mane and then stood back, horrified.

The little pony tilted his head and looked at Emma from beneath his bushy forelock. Two bright eyes twinkled like diamonds in the afternoon sunshine.

"Oh, no," she gasped. "You're not my Sheltie. You're Topper!" Emma was certain of it.

The two ponies may have looked identical to anyone else, but not to Emma. There was something about Topper that wasn't Sheltie. She just *knew* this wasn't her little pony.

Topper gave a soft whicker, as if to say,

"It's not my fault!" But Emma burst into tears as she ran back to the house.

For a moment, she had forgotten that Mom had gone out. But then Emma remembered her mom wouldn't be back until at least six o'clock. She stood in the kitchen and wiped her eyes.

"This is no time for crying," she told herself. "If Topper's *here*, then where is Sheltie?" Emma guessed that somehow the two ponies had gotten mixed up again and been swapped. Sheltie must be tethered somewhere, otherwise he would have come back to the paddock on his own. He was always there, waiting for Emma when she came home from school.

Emma had made up her mind. The campers must have found Sheltie and mistaken him for Topper again. Toyah had said they were moving from the fields very soon.

"There's only one thing to do!" Emma told herself. And there wasn't a moment to lose. If she didn't act quickly, Emma knew she might never see Sheltie again.

Chapter Eight

Emma left a note for Mom and Dad to let them know what had happened. Then she rushed outside to saddle up Topper.

But the circus pony wasn't as willing as Sheltie. He danced around while Emma tacked him up. He nudged her bottom when she tightened the girth strap. He clamped his jaws shut when she tried to ease in the bit. And then he took hold

of the reins in his mouth and wouldn't let go.

At last, Emma was up in the saddle and in control, or at least she thought she was. But Topper had other ideas.

When Emma squeezed with her legs and gave the command to "walk on," Topper decided on a funny little hop and pranced sideways through the gate and out into the road.

"Come on, Topper. Behave!" said Emma sternly. But the mischievous circus pony continued sideways up the road just like a crab.

Emma was really annoyed. She pushed her seat deep and hard into the saddle and pulled in the reins taut. Then she firmly gripped Topper's sides with her legs. Emma meant business now! And the pony responded by straightening himself up.

"Come on, Topper," pleaded Emma. "I know you're very clever and doing funny things, but I need your help to find Sheltie. And I need it now!"

Suddenly, the circus pony seemed to understand and took off down the road at a fast pace.

The quickest way to the North Field was up through the woods behind Barrow Hill. There was a shortcut across the top meadow, but Emma decided to keep to the bridle paths. The last thing she wanted was for Topper to bolt away across a field.

As they skirted Barrow Hill and were climbing up through the woods, Emma began to worry. What if the campers had left ages ago? Emma would have no way of knowing which direction they had taken.

Fresh tears welled in her eyes as she rode Topper through the woods. The thought of never seeing Sheltie again was unbearable. She blinked the tears back as best she could, not daring to let go of the reins for a second. The trees passed in a hazy blur, then opened out on to the fields in a blaze of sunshine.

Still holding the reins, Emma wiped her eyes with her sleeve. Then her heart sank.

Emma could see for miles in all directions. And the North Field was completely empty.

Oh, no! The words screamed inside Emma's head. But when she opened her mouth, no sound came out.

Emma couldn't believe what had happened. The campers had moved on. They must have taken Sheltie with them.

Emma didn't know what to do. But she had to do something. She couldn't just sit there while Sheltie was being taken farther and farther away.

"Which way should I go?" she cried. But there was no one to hear her except Topper. The circus pony turned his head around and tried to nibble Emma's foot in the stirrup.

She pulled his head up with the reins.

"If it was *you* that was missing," cried Emma, "Sheltie would help find you. He'd sniff the air and know exactly which way you'd gone. He'd smell your scent and lead me to you."

Emma found herself taking comfort in stroking Topper's neck. "Can't you do the same, boy?" she asked. "Can't you find Sheltie?"

At the mention of Sheltie's name, Topper pricked up his ears. Emma didn't know whether he understood or whether he caught a scent on the sudden breeze. But the little circus pony lurched forward and carried Emma east across the fields, toward the main road. He flew along with his tail streaming out behind.

Emma rode like the wind and put her trust in Topper. She didn't know how sure-footed he was, but she had no choice. She had to rescue Sheltie.

They rode across the fields, over a rise, and down a basin slope that led toward the main road. Suddenly Emma saw a small group of vans and trailers ahead. She held her breath. An old camper with a funny-looking tin chimney poking out of its roof led the line of vehicles.

It was the campers. They were crawling along, but they had almost reached the main road.

Emma pulled Topper to a halt on the summit of the rise and stood up in the stirrups, yelling at the top of her voice. But no one seemed to hear.

"Come on, Topper." She reined him into a gallop and flew down the slope.

"Stop!" yelled Emma as they thundered along. "Stop!"

And luckily, this time, someone in a coach at the back heard, because the line of vans and trailers came to a sudden halt.

Toyah jumped out of one of the vans as Emma rode up on Topper.

"What is it?" she asked. "What's the matter? Is something wrong?"

"Yes!" panted Emma, jumping from the saddle. "It's Sheltie!"

"Sheltie?" Toyah looked puzzled. "What's wrong with Sheltie? He looks fine to me!" She looked Topper up and down.

"This isn't Sheltie!" shouted Emma. "This is Topper! They've gotten mixed up again. I've got *your* pony and you've got Sheltie!"

Toyah looked very surprised. Then she looked very worried.

"Oh, no!" she groaned. "I don't know how to tell you this."

"What's wrong?" asked Emma anxiously.

Toyah lowered her eyes and explained. "Well," she began. "As you know, Topper can be quite a handful. And as we're always on the move, we thought it would be better if Topper had an owner who could give him more time and keep him in one place. Someone with a little boy or girl who could love and look after him properly."

Emma listened to all this with her mouth open. "What are you saying, exactly?" she asked. "Where's Sheltie?"

"We didn't know it was Sheltie when we found him," said Toyah. "We thought it was Topper. And we've given him away."

Chapter Nine

"Given him away!" cried Emma. She couldn't believe it. "Given him away! Who have you given Sheltie to?"

"We don't know where she lives, but she was a nice, friendly lady," said Toyah sheepishly. "We got to talking to her on the fields. She said she knew *exactly* the right owner. I'm really sorry, but we didn't know it was your pony we had given away; we thought it was Topper."

Emma's face crumpled as she burst into tears. It sounded as though she had lost Sheltie forever.

Toyah's mother got out of the van and joined them. She listened as Toyah explained what had happened.

"I don't suppose you'd even want to think about keeping Topper instead, would you?" she asked.

"No! I wouldn't," cried Emma. She didn't mean to sound rude, but she was very upset. And *very* angry. "I don't want Topper. I want my Sheltie." Poor Emma. All she could do was stand there crying.

The woman put a comforting arm around Emma's shoulders. "Don't worry, dear," she said. "We'll help you find your pony." Then she put her fingers to her

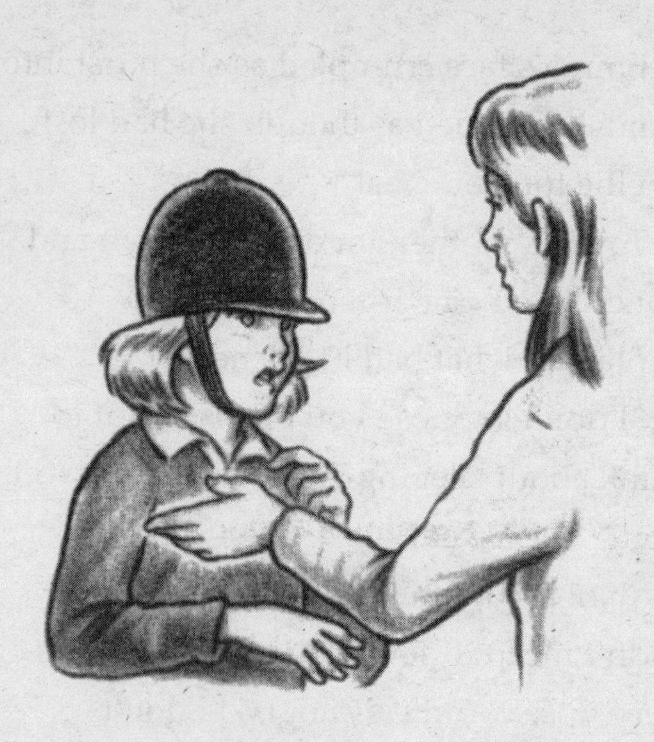

mouth and blew a series of short, sharp whistles.

Immediately, three teenage boys appeared.

"These are my sons," she said proudly. "They'll find Sheltie for you on their bikes."

Emma watched as the boys rolled three small motorbikes out of a nearby trailer. The engines sounded like noisy lawn mowers as they started the bikes and rode off to check on all the houses and farms.

"And now, I think I'd better take you home," Toyah's mom added, steering Emma toward a brightly colored van. "There's nothing more you can do here."

Emma didn't argue. What Toyah's mom said was true. There was nothing that Emma *could* do. Sheltie could be anywhere. And all Emma could do was go home and wait.

She sat quietly in the van as it rumbled along, feeling that her heart was about to break. Life without Sheltie would be unbearable. Emma had never felt so sad.

Tears flowed down her cheeks for the entire journey. And when the van pulled up in the road outside the house, Emma's face was all red and puffy.

She blinked away the tears from her eyes to look at Sheltie's empty paddock. She couldn't really bear to look, but she felt she just *had* to.

Then Emma gasped. Her misty eyes seemed to be playing tricks. Through her tears, Emma thought she saw Sheltie standing by the paddock gate. Then she saw Mom and Dad with Mrs. Linney. Emma's stomach turned a complete somersault as she jumped out of the van.

"Sheltie!" cried Emma. "It *is* you!" She wasn't seeing things after all.

The little pony tossed back his head and

greeted Emma with a noisy snicker of welcoming snorts. She threw her arms around his furry neck and buried her face in his shaggy mane. The hair was coarse and smelled of hay. It *was* Sheltie. And he was there in Emma's arms. She felt like she never, ever wanted to let go.

"That's the woman we gave your pony to," said Toyah's mom. She pointed toward Mrs. Linney as she climbed out of the van.

Mrs. Linney smiled and explained what had happened. "I was hiking up in the fields," she told Toyah's mom, "and when I saw you with Sheltie I guessed that there had been another mix-up. Mr. Crock told me all about the first time that Topper was mistaken for Sheltie. But although Topper is Sheltie's double, like Emma, I'd know the real Sheltie anywhere. After all, he used to be *my* pony."

"But why didn't you explain?" asked Toyah's mom.

"I was going to," answered Mrs. Linney, "but then we got to talking and you offered

to give me Sheltie, or Topper as you thought. And since you were happy to give the pony away to a good home, I thought it would be easier if I just took him home. All I knew was that I had to get Sheltie back to Emma."

"So when you said you knew just the right owner, you meant Emma here?"

"Exactly!" Mrs. Linney smiled. "But I still promise I'll find a good home for the real Topper, just as I said I would."

"So everything's turned out all right in the end," said Toyah.

"No it hasn't," groaned Mom.

Everyone turned to look at her.

"Why? What's wrong?" asked Dad.

Mom gave a weak grin and pointed to Emma's backpack.

"The flyers," she said. "I promised Mrs. Hamilton they would all be delivered this afternoon."

"Sorry, Mom." Emma gulped. "I forgot all about them."

"It doesn't matter, Emma. I'll get Dad to volunteer!"

Dad raised his eyebrows and grinned.

"I've got a better idea," said Toyah's mom, smiling broadly. She took a cell phone from her pocket and punched in some numbers. "Jason," she said, "call in the boys and get here as soon as you can. It's another emergency. There's an important errand that needs running. Meet me in the road down from town to the farm. Over and out."

Within five minutes the drone of motorbikes could be heard buzzing down

the road. Sheltie pulled his head from Emma's arms and pricked up his ears as Jason and his brothers skidded to a halt outside the house.

"Urgent flyers to be delivered, boys," said their mother.

"Where to?" they asked.

"All over Little Applewood," she told them.

"But we don't know the area *that* well," said Jason.

"I can help you," announced Mrs. Linney suddenly. She picked up Emma's backpack and, with a great effort, swung her leg over the seat behind Jason. "I haven't been on one of these for years," she said with a grin. "And I can collect Topper when we've finished and walk him home."

Then they were gone in a cloud of dust,

with Mrs. Linney wobbling like jelly on the back of the motorbike.

Emma burst out laughing. Sheltie curled back his lips as though he was laughing, too. Then he blew a long, low snort that sounded just like a motorbike and made Emma laugh even more.